Donald TRUMP

Tamara L. Britton

Big Buddy Books
An Imprint of Abdo Publishing

Published by Abdo Publishing, a division of ABDO, PO Box 398166, Minneapolis, Minnesota 55439.

Printed in the United States of America, North Mankato, Minnesota
112024
012025

Cover Photograph: Wikimedia Commons
Interior Photographs: Alamy (pp. 9); AP Images (pp. 7, 15, 19, 21); Getty Images (p. 6, 7, 13, 23, 25, 27, 29); Wikimedia Commons (pp. 5, 6, 7, 11, 17)

Editors: Krissy Sterling and Lauri Nelson
Series Designers: Candice Keimig and Laura Graphenteen

Library of Congress Control Number: 2023949325

Publisher's Cataloging-in-Publication Data

Names: Britton, Tamara L., author.
Title: Donald Trump / by Tamara L. Britton
Description: Minneapolis, Minnesota : Abdo Publishing, 2025 | Series: Presidents of the United States | Includes online resources and index.
Identifiers: ISBN 9781098294861 (lib. bdg.) | ISBN 9798384914594 (ebook)
Subjects: LCSH: Trump, Donald, 1946---Juvenile literature. | Presidents--Biography--Juvenile literature. | Presidents--United States--History--Juvenile literature. | Legislators--United States--Biography--Juvenile literature. | Politics and government--Biography--Juvenile literature.
Classification: DDC 973.932092--dc23

CONTENTS

DONALD TRUMP 4
TIMELINE 6
FAMILY BUSINESS 8
SCHOOL DAYS 10
EARLY SUCCESS 12
SURPRISE NOMINEE 14
PRESIDENT TRUMP 16
MORE CHALLENGES 20
ELECTION 2020 22
HISTORIC COMEBACK 26

Office of the President 30
Presidents and Their Terms 34
Glossary 38
Websites 39
Index 40

DONALD TRUMP

Donald Trump was the forty-fifth and forty-seventh US president. He is the second president whose terms were not in a row.

In 2016, Trump was elected president. Four years later, he lost a close election. Then, in 2024, Trump was elected president for a second time.

President Trump worked to control **immigration** and to improve US trade and tax policies. But, he faced many challenges. He led the nation during the COVID-19 **pandemic**. He was **impeached** twice. And, he was the first president to be **convicted** of crimes.

TIMELINE

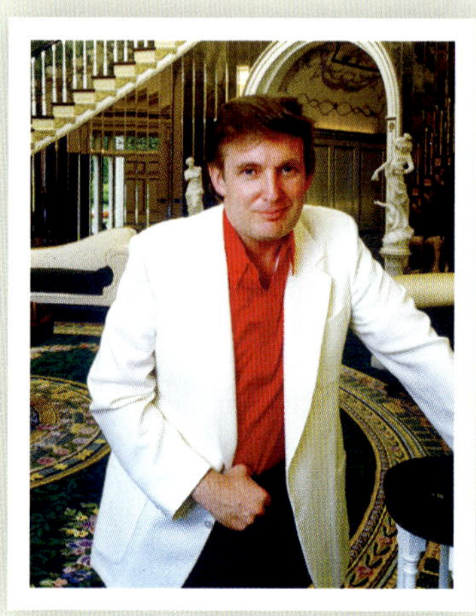

1946
On June 14, Donald Trump was born in New York City.

1968
Trump **graduated** from college.

1983
Trump Tower opened.

2004–2015
Trump starred in the reality TV series *The* ***Apprentice*** and *The* ***Celebrity*** *Apprentice.*

2017

Trump was sworn in as the forty-fifth president of the US.

2019

Trump was **impeached**. The COVID-19 **pandemic** began.

2021

On January 13, Trump was impeached for the second time. His term ended on January 20.

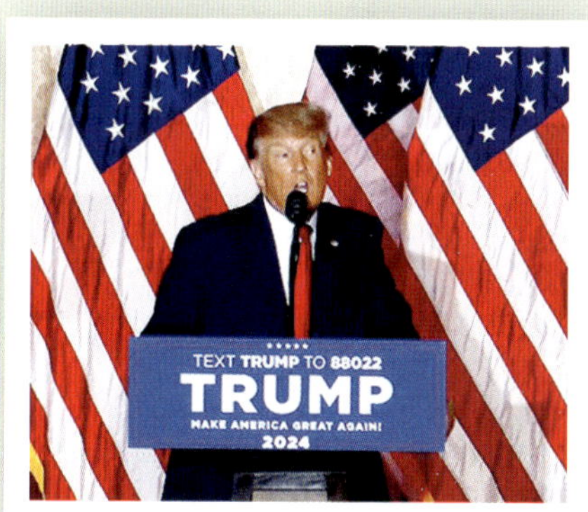

2024

On July 13, a man shot Trump at a campaign gathering. On November 5, Trump was reelected to become the forty-seventh US president.

FAMILY BUSINESS

Donald John Trump was born on June 14, 1946, in Queens, New York. His parents were Frederick C. and Mary Trump. Fred ran a construction and **real estate** business. Mary was a homemaker. Donald had two sisters and two brothers.

Fast FACTS

BORN: June 14, 1946

WIVES: Ivana Zelníčková (1949–2022), Marla Maples (1963–), Melania Knauss (1970–)

CHILDREN: five

POLITICAL PARTY: Republican

AGE AT INAUGURATIONS: 70, 78

YEARS SERVED: 2017–2021, 2025-

VICE PRESIDENTS: Mike Pence, JD Vance

Trump with his parents

SCHOOL DAYS

Donald attended the Kew-Forest School in Forest Hills, New York. When Donald was 13, he entered the New York Military Academy in Cornwall-on-Hudson, New York. Donald **graduated** in 1964.

Later that year, he entered Fordham **University** in New York City. In 1966, he transferred to the University of Pennsylvania. There, Donald studied **economics** at the Wharton School. Donald graduated in 1968. Then he went to work for his father's company.

At New York Military Academy, Donald was captain of the baseball team.

EARLY SUCCESS

In 1971, Trump took control of the family business. In 1983, he opened Trump Tower on New York City's Fifth Avenue. At the time it was the tallest all-glass building in Manhattan.

Trump was a successful businessman. But during a **recession** in the early 1990s, his properties lost value. He worked hard to grow his businesses again.

The **economy** slowly improved. Trump was soon ready for a new challenge. In 2004, he began starring in a TV show called *The **Apprentice***. The program's success led to *The **Celebrity** Apprentice* in 2008.

Trump's mansion in Greenwich, Connecticut, had a three-story entry, eight bedrooms, and two swimming pools.

SURPRISE NOMINEE

In June 2015, Trump announced he was running for president. On July 19, he received the **Republican** Party's **nomination**. Indiana governor Mike Pence was his **running mate**.

Hillary Clinton was the **Democratic** Party's nominee. Her running mate was Virginia senator Tim Kaine. Unlike Trump, Clinton had a lot of **political** experience. She was favored to win. But on November 8, 2016, Trump was voted to be the nation's forty-fifth president.

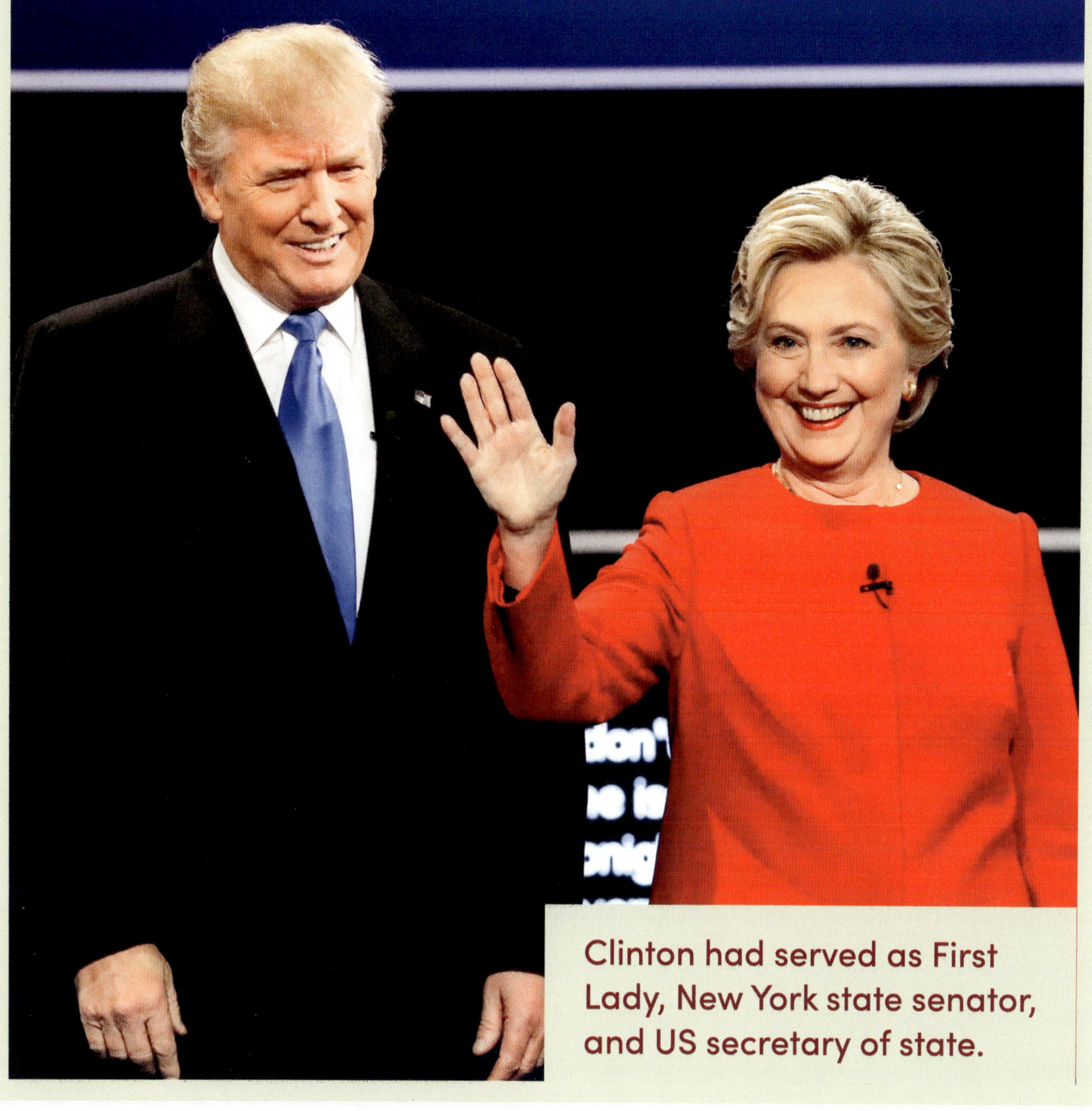

Clinton had served as First Lady, New York state senator, and US secretary of state.

PRESIDENT TRUMP

Trump took office on January 20, 2017. That December, he signed the Tax Cuts and Jobs Act. This bill reduced taxes on **corporations** and gave tax benefits to individuals and families.

President Trump signed the First Step Act in 2018. This law improved prisons and made communities safer. Imprisoned men and women got job training. They got help rejoining society after they had served their time. These steps increased public safety.

Trump was sworn in with two Bibles. One belonged to Abraham Lincoln. The other was a gift from Trump's mother.

The US Space Force was established by President Trump in 2019. It became the sixth branch of the US Armed Forces. The Space Force protects the nation's interests in space. It was the first new military service since the US Air Force was created in 1947.

In August 2019, Trump called Ukraine's president, Volodymyr Zelensky. He asked Zelensky to look into former US vice president Joe Biden. On December 18, the House of Representatives **impeached** Trump for this action. But on February 5, 2020, the Senate found him not guilty.

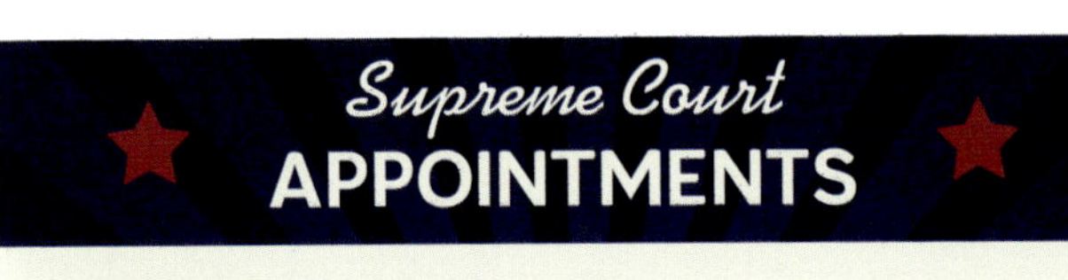

NEIL GORSUCH: 2017
BRETT KAVANAUGH: 2018
AMY CONEY BARRETT: 2020

President TRUMP'S CABINET

First Term

January 20, 2017–January 20, 2021

- **STATE:** Rex W. Tillerson
  Mike Pompeo (from April 26, 2018)
- **TREASURY:** Steven Mnuchin
- **DEFENSE:** James Mattis
  Mark T. Esper (from July 23, 2019)
  Christopher C. Miller (from November 9, 2020)
- **ATTORNEY GENERAL:** Jeff Sessions
  William Barr (from February 14, 2019)
  Jeffrey A. Rosen (acting from December 24, 2020)
- **INTERIOR:** Ryan Zinke
  David Bernhardt (from April 11, 2019)
- **AGRICULTURE:** Sonny Perdue
- **COMMERCE:** Wilbur L. Ross Jr.
- **LABOR:** R. Alexander Acosta
  Eugene Scalia (from September 30, 2019)
- **HEALTH AND HUMAN SERVICES:** Thomas Price
  Alex M. Azar II (from January 29, 2018)
- **HOUSING AND URBAN DEVELOPMENT:**
  Benjamin S. Carson Sr.
- **TRANSPORTATION:** Elaine L. Chao
  Steven G. Bradbury (acting from January 12, 2021)
- **ENERGY:** Rick Perry
  Dan Brouillette (from December 4, 2019)
- **EDUCATION:** Betsy DeVos
  Mick Zais (acting from January 8, 2021)
- **VETERANS AFFAIRS:** David J. Shulkin
  Robert Wilkie (from July 30, 2018)
- **HOMELAND SECURITY:** John F. Kelly
  Kirstjen M. Nielsen (from December 5, 2017)
  Chad F. Wolf (acting from November 13, 2019)
  Pete Gaynor (acting from January 12, 2021)

MORE CHALLENGES

In December 2019, a new virus appeared in China. It caused an illness called COVID-19. It soon spread throughout the world.

Efforts to stop it hurt the **economy**. So Trump signed the Coronavirus Aid, Relief, and Economic Security (CARES) Act on March 27, 2020. It gave money to help individuals and small businesses.

The country also faced protests calling for an end to **racism** and violence against Black people. The protests spread around the world.

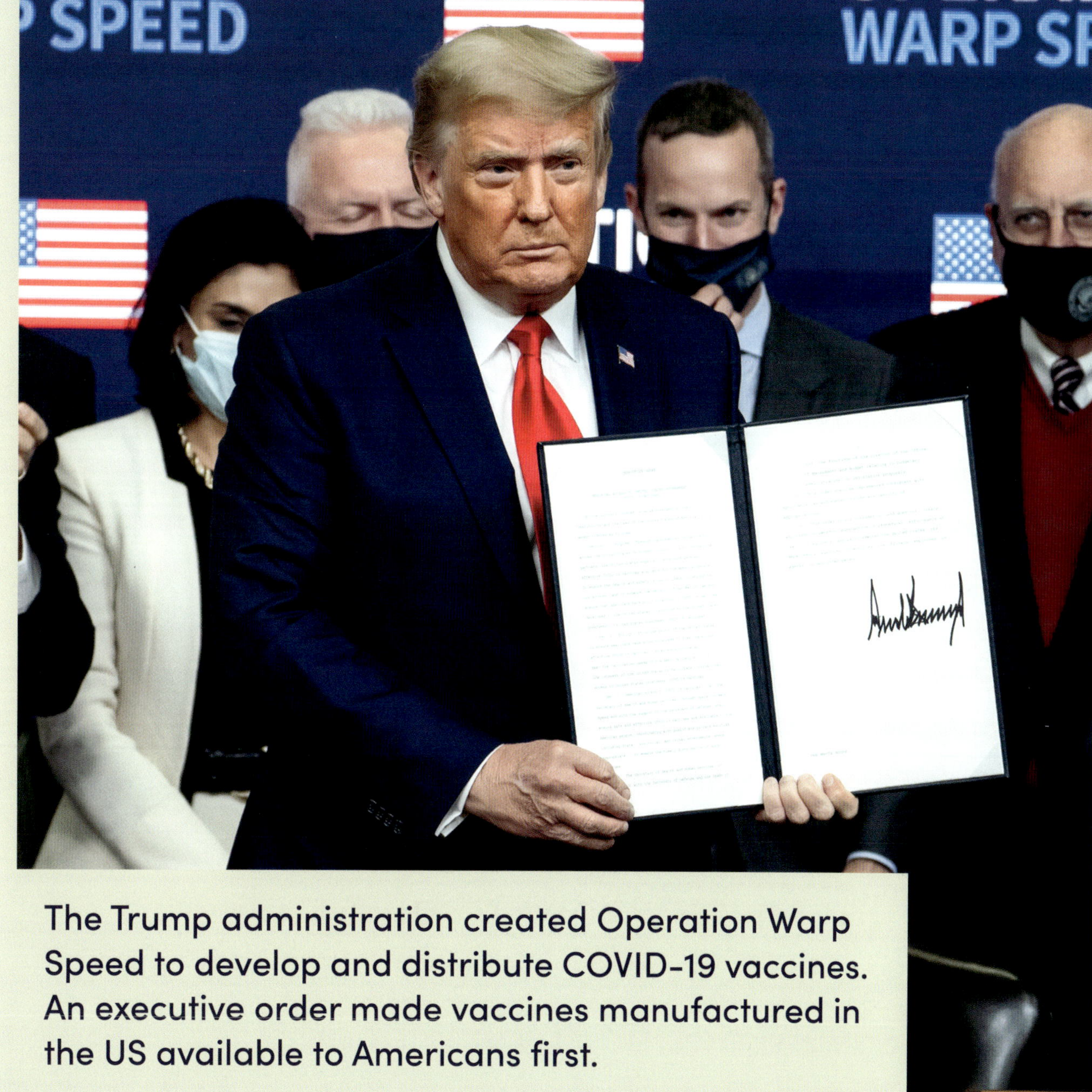

The Trump administration created Operation Warp Speed to develop and distribute COVID-19 vaccines. An executive order made vaccines manufactured in the US available to Americans first.

ELECTION 2020

On September 18, 2020, US Supreme Court Justice Ruth Bader Ginsburg died. President Trump chose Amy Coney Barrett to replace her. Barrett was the fifth woman to serve on the nation's highest court.

During this time, Trump also campaigned for reelection. Joe Biden was the **Democratic nominee**. California senator Kamala Harris was Biden's **running mate**.

Due to COVID-19, more than 100 million people voted early or by mail. On Election Day, both Trump and Biden received a record number of votes. On November 7, 2020, Biden and Harris were declared the winners.

President Trump nominated Amy Coney Barrett *(right)* on September 26, 2020. She made history as the first mother of school-aged children to serve on the US Supreme Court.

Trump believed there had been cheating in how the election votes were counted. Many Americans agreed. Results in several states were challenged. But no cheating was found.

On January 6, 2021, a protest in Washington, DC, supported these challenges. Some protesters illegally entered the US Capitol. They wanted to stop Congress from making the election results official. Others fought with police. Trump later agreed to a peaceful handover of power.

On January 13, the House of Representatives **impeached** Trump for **inciting insurrection**. His term ended the following week. The Senate found Trump not guilty on February 13, 2021.

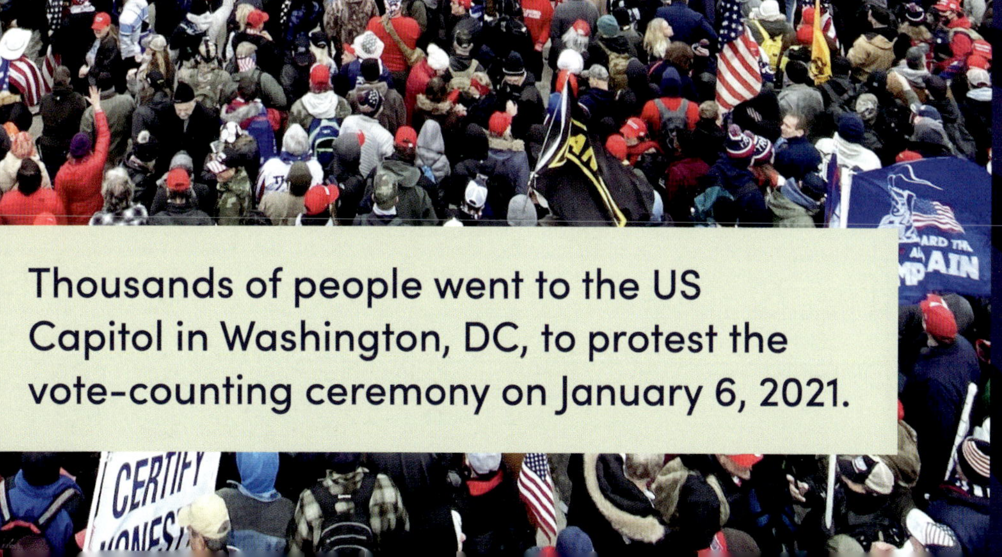

Thousands of people went to the US Capitol in Washington, DC, to protest the vote-counting ceremony on January 6, 2021.

HISTORIC COMEBACK

Trump remained active in **politics**. In November 2022, he announced he would run for president again in 2024.

Some states thought Trump should not be allowed to become president again. The US Supreme Court ruled that Trump could not be kept off **ballots**.

In May 2024, Trump was **convicted** on 34 counts of changing his business records. He did this to hide illegal payments made during the 2016 election. He became the first US president to be convicted of crimes.

Trump spoke at the Mar-a-Lago Club in Palm Beach, Florida, to announce his plan for reelection.

Trump's struggles continued as he ran for reelection. A man shot him at a **political** event in July. Trump's right ear was hit by a bullet.

Trump's slogan was "Make America Great Again." He promised to protect the borders and fix the **economy**. He also wanted to make America the greatest **energy** producer in the world.

On November 5, 2024, more than 142 million people voted. Trump and his **running mate**, JD Vance, won the election against the **Democratic** Party candidate Kamala Harris. It was a historic comeback.

Trump won the popular vote and 312 electoral votes in the 2024 election.

Trump with his wife Melania *(left)* and son Barron *(center)*, at the Palm Beach Convention Center on election night

OFFICE OF THE PRESIDENT

Branches of Government

The US government has three branches. They are the executive, legislative, and judicial branches. Each branch has some power over the others. This is called a system of checks and balances.

★ Executive Branch

The executive branch enforces laws. It is made up of the president, the vice president, and the president's cabinet. The president represents the United States around the world. He or she also signs bills into law and leads the military.

★ Legislative Branch

The legislative branch makes laws, maintains the military, and regulates trade. It also has the power to declare war. This branch includes the Senate and the House of Representatives. Together, these two houses form Congress.

★ Judicial Branch

The judicial branch interprets laws. It is made up of district courts, courts of appeals, and the Supreme Court. District courts try cases. Sometimes people disagree with a trial's outcome. Then he or she may appeal. If a court of appeals supports the ruling, a person may appeal to the Supreme Court.

Qualifications for Office

To be president, a candidate must be at least 35 years old. The person must be a natural-born US citizen. He or she must also have lived in the United States for at least 14 years.

Electoral College

The US presidential election is an indirect election. Voters from each state choose electors. These electors represent their state in the Electoral College. Each elector has one electoral vote. Electors cast their vote for the candidate with the highest number of votes from people in their state. A candidate must receive the majority of Electoral College votes to win.

Term of Office

Each president may be elected to two four-year terms. The presidential election is held on the Tuesday after the first Monday in November. The president is sworn in on January 20 of the following year. At that time, he or she takes the oath of office.

It states:

> I do solemnly swear (or affirm) that I will faithfully execute the office of President of the United States, and will to the best of my ability, preserve, protect and defend the Constitution of the United States.

Line of Succession

The Presidential Succession Act of 1947 states who becomes president if the president cannot serve. The vice president is first in the line. Next are the Speaker of the House and the President Pro Tempore of the Senate. It may happen that none of these individuals is able to serve. Then the office falls to the president's cabinet members. They would take office in the order in which each department was created:

1. **Vice President**
2. **Speaker of the House**
3. **President Pro Tempore of the Senate**
4. **Secretary of State**
5. **Secretary of the Treasury**
6. **Secretary of Defense**
7. **Attorney General**
8. **Secretary of the Interior**
9. **Secretary of Agriculture**
10. **Secretary of Commerce**
11. **Secretary of Labor**
12. **Secretary of Health and Human Services**
13. **Secretary of Housing and Urban Development**
14. **Secretary of Transportation**
15. **Secretary of Energy**
16. **Secretary of Education**
17. **Secretary of Veterans Affairs**
18. **Secretary of Homeland Security**

Modern-Day Benefits

- ★ While in office, the president receives a salary. It is $400,000 per year. He or she lives in the White House. The president also has 24-hour Secret Service protection.
- ★ The president may travel on a Boeing 747 jet. This special jet is called Air Force One. It can hold 76 passengers. It has kitchens, a dining room, sleeping areas, and more. Air Force One can fly halfway around the world before needing to refuel. It can even refuel in flight!
- ★ When the president travels by car, he or she uses Cadillac One. It is a Cadillac that has been modified. The car has heavy armor and communications systems. The president may even take Cadillac One along when visiting other countries.
- ★ The president also travels on a helicopter. It is called Marine One. It may also be taken along when the president visits other countries.
- ★ Sometimes the president needs to get away with family and friends. Camp David is the official presidential retreat. It is located in Maryland. The US Navy maintains the retreat. The US Marine Corps keeps it secure. The camp offers swimming, tennis, golf, and hiking.
- ★ When the president leaves office, he or she receives lifetime Secret Service protection. He or she also receives a yearly pension that may be modified by Congress every year. In 2023, the pension amount was $226,300. The former president also receives money for office space, supplies, and staff.

PRESIDENTS AND THEIR TERMS

PRESIDENT	PARTY	TOOK OFFICE	LEFT OFFICE	TERMS SERVED	VICE PRESIDENT
George Washington	None	April 30, 1789	March 4, 1797	Two	John Adams
John Adams	Federalist	March 4, 1797	March 4, 1801	One	Thomas Jefferson
Thomas Jefferson	Democratic-Republican	March 4, 1801	March 4, 1809	Two	Aaron Burr, George Clinton
James Madison	Democratic-Republican	March 4, 1809	March 4, 1817	Two	George Clinton, Elbridge Gerry
James Monroe	Democratic-Republican	March 4, 1817	March 4, 1825	Two	Daniel D. Tompkins
John Quincy Adams	Democratic-Republican	March 4, 1825	March 4, 1829	One	John C. Calhoun
Andrew Jackson	Democrat	March 4, 1829	March 4, 1837	Two	John C. Calhoun, Martin Van Buren
Martin Van Buren	Democrat	March 4, 1837	March 4, 1841	One	Richard M. Johnson
William H. Harrison	Whig	March 4, 1841	April 4, 1841	Died During First Term	John Tyler
John Tyler	Whig	April 6, 1841	March 4, 1845	Completed Harrison's Term	Office Vacant
James K. Polk	Democrat	March 4, 1845	March 4, 1849	One	George M. Dallas
Zachary Taylor	Whig	March 5, 1849	July 9, 1850	Died During First Term	Millard Fillmore

PRESIDENT	PARTY	TOOK OFFICE	LEFT OFFICE	TERMS SERVED	VICE PRESIDENT
Millard Fillmore	Whig	July 10, 1850	March 4, 1853	Completed Taylor's Term	Office Vacant
Franklin Pierce	Democrat	March 4, 1853	March 4, 1857	One	William R.D. King
James Buchanan	Democrat	March 4, 1857	March 4, 1861	One	John C. Breckinridge
Abraham Lincoln	Republican	March 4, 1861	April 15, 1865	Served One Term, Died During Second Term	Hannibal Hamlin, Andrew Johnson
Andrew Johnson	Democrat	April 15, 1865	March 4, 1869	Completed Lincoln's Second Term	Office Vacant
Ulysses S. Grant	Republican	March 4, 1869	March 4, 1877	Two	Schuyler Colfax, Henry Wilson
Rutherford B. Hayes	Republican	March 3, 1877	March 4, 1881	One	William A. Wheeler
James A. Garfield	Republican	March 4, 1881	September 19, 1881	Died During First Term	Chester Arthur
Chester Arthur	Republican	September 20, 1881	March 4, 1885	Completed Garfield's Term	Office Vacant
Grover Cleveland	Democrat	March 4, 1885	March 4, 1889	One	Thomas A. Hendricks
Benjamin Harrison	Republican	March 4, 1889	March 4, 1893	One	Levi P. Morton
Grover Cleveland	Democrat	March 4, 1893	March 4, 1897	One	Adlai E. Stevenson
William McKinley	Republican	March 4, 1897	September 14, 1901	Served One Term, Died During Second Term	Garret A. Hobart, Theodore Roosevelt

PRESIDENT	PARTY	TOOK OFFICE	LEFT OFFICE	TERMS SERVED	VICE PRESIDENT
Theodore Roosevelt	Republican	September 14, 1901	March 4, 1909	Completed McKinley's Second Term, Served One Term	Office Vacant, Charles Fairbanks
William Taft	Republican	March 4, 1909	March 4, 1913	One	James S. Sherman
Woodrow Wilson	Democrat	March 4, 1913	March 4, 1921	Two	Thomas R. Marshall
Warren G. Harding	Republican	March 4, 1921	August 2, 1923	Died During First Term	Calvin Coolidge
Calvin Coolidge	Republican	August 3, 1923	March 4, 1929	Completed Harding's Term, Served One Term	Office Vacant, Charles Dawes
Herbert Hoover	Republican	March 4, 1929	March 4, 1933	One	Charles Curtis
Franklin D. Roosevelt	Democrat	March 4, 1933	April 12, 1945	Served Three Terms, Died During Fourth Term	John Nance Garner, Henry A. Wallace, Harry S. Truman
Harry S. Truman	Democrat	April 12, 1945	January 20, 1953	Completed Roosevelt's Fourth Term, Served One Term	Office Vacant, Alben Barkley
Dwight D. Eisenhower	Republican	January 20, 1953	January 20, 1961	Two	Richard Nixon
John F. Kennedy	Democrat	January 20, 1961	November 22, 1963	Died During First Term	Lyndon B. Johnson
Lyndon B. Johnson	Democrat	November 22, 1963	January 20, 1969	Completed Kennedy's Term, Served One Term	Office Vacant, Hubert H. Humphrey
Richard Nixon	Republican	January 20, 1969	August 9, 1974	Completed First Term, Resigned During Second Term	Spiro T. Agnew, Gerald Ford

PRESIDENT	PARTY	TOOK OFFICE	LEFT OFFICE	TERMS SERVED	VICE PRESIDENT
Gerald Ford	Republican	August 9, 1974	January 20, 1977	Completed Nixon's Second Term	Nelson A. Rockefeller
Jimmy Carter	Democrat	January 20, 1977	January 20, 1981	One	Walter Mondale
Ronald Reagan	Republican	January 20, 1981	January 20, 1989	Two	George H.W. Bush
George H.W. Bush	Republican	January 20, 1989	January 20, 1993	One	Dan Quayle
Bill Clinton	Democrat	January 20, 1993	January 20, 2001	Two	Al Gore
George W. Bush	Republican	January 20, 2001	January 20, 2009	Two	Dick Cheney
Barack Obama	Democrat	January 20, 2009	January 20, 2017	Two	Joe Biden
Donald Trump	Republican	January 20, 2017	January 20, 2021	One	Mike Pence
Joe Biden	Democrat	January 20, 2021	January 20, 2025	One	Kamala Harris
Donald Trump	Republican	January 20, 2025			JD Vance

★ ★ WRITE TO THE *President* ★ ★

You may write to the president at:
The White House
1600 Pennsylvania Avenue NW
Washington, DC 20500

You may e-mail the president at:
www.whitehouse.gov/contact

"We must reclaim our country's destiny and dream big and bold and daring."

Donald Trump

GLOSSARY

apprentice (uh-PREHN-tiss)—a person who learns a trade or craft from a skilled worker.

ballot—a sheet of paper that lists the choices during an election.

celebrity (suh-LEB-ruh-tee)—a famous person.

convict—to find or prove to have done something illegal.

corporation—a large business or organization that follows a specific purpose.

Democrat—a member of the Democratic political party.

economy—the way that a country produces, sells, and buys goods and services. The study of the economy is economics.

energy—the ability to do work; usable power such as heat or electricity.

graduate (GRA-juh-wayt)—to complete a level of schooling.

immigration—the act of leaving one's home and settling in a new country.

impeach—to charge a public official with misconduct in office.

incite—to move to action.

insurrection—a usually violent attempt to take control of a government.

nominate—to name as a possible winner. A person who is nominated is a nominee.

nonconsecutive—not in order or following continuously.

pandemic—worldwide spread of a disease that can affect most people.

politics—the art or science of government. Something referring to politics is political. A person who is active in politics is a politician.

racism (RAY-sih-zuhm)—the belief that one race is better than another.

real estate—the business of selling buildings and land.

recession (rih-SEH-shuhn)—a period of time when business activity slows.

Republican—a member of the Republican political party.

running mate—someone running for vice president with another person running for president in an election.

university—a school that offers courses leading to a degree.

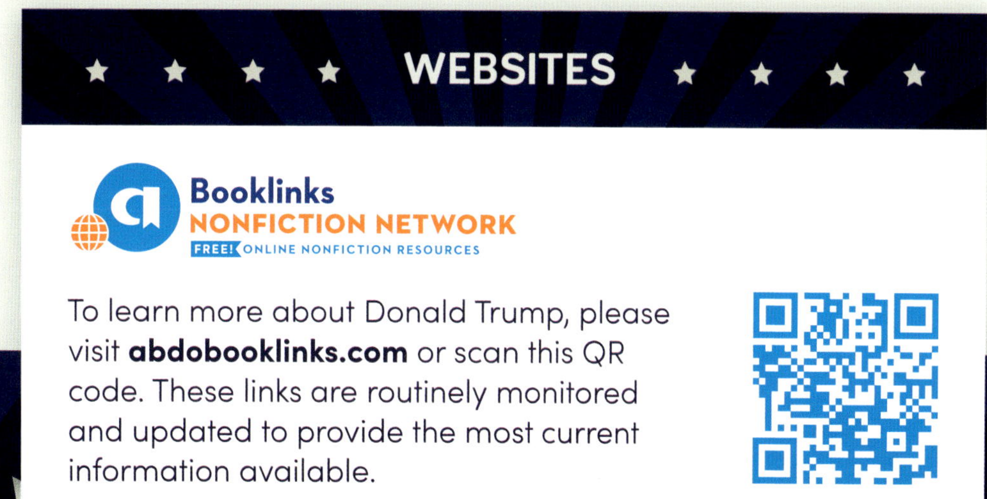

To learn more about Donald Trump, please visit **abdobooklinks.com** or scan this QR code. These links are routinely monitored and updated to provide the most current information available.

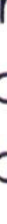

INDEX

Apprentice, The **6, 12**
Barrett, Amy Coney **18, 22**
Biden, Joe **18, 22**
birth **6, 8**
Celebrity Apprentice, The **6, 12**
Clinton, Hillary **14, 15**
Coronavirus Aid, Relief, and Economic Security (CARES) Act **20**
COVID-19 pandemic **4, 7, 20, 21, 22**
crimes **4, 26**
Democratic Party **14, 22, 28**
economy **12, 20, 28**
education **10, 11**
elections **4, 7, 14, 22, 24, 26, 28**
family **8, 12, 17, 29**
First Step Act **16**
Ginsburg, Ruth Bader **22**
Harris, Kamala **22, 28**
House of Representatives, US **18, 24**
impeachments **4, 7, 18, 24**
inauguration **8, 16, 17**
Pence, Mike **8, 14**
policies **4, 16**
protests **20, 24, 25**
real estate **8, 12**
Republican Party **8, 14**
Senate, US **18, 24**
Tax Cuts and Jobs Act **16**
Ukraine **18**
US Space Force **18**
US Supreme Court **18, 22, 26**
Vance, JD **8, 28**
Washington, DC **24, 25**
Zelensky, Volodymyr **18**